Dad

Mum

Lu

Lucy

m

Dad

Mum

Lu

Lucy

Will

Will

n

The Quigleys

The Quigleys

Simon Mason

Illustrated by Helen Stephens

David Fickling Books

OXFORD · NEW YORK

A DAVID FICKLING BOOK

Published by David Fickling Books
an imprint of Random House Children's Books
a division of Random House, Inc.
1540 Broadway
New York, New York 10036

Text copyright © 2002 by Simon Mason
Illustrations copyright © 2002 by Helen Stephens

Published simultaneously in Canada by Random House of Canada Limited,
Toronto, and in Great Britain by David Fickling Books,
a division of Random House Children's Books

www.randomhouse.com/kids

Library of Congress Cataloging-in-Publication Data is available upon request.
ISBN 0-385-75006-4
Printed in the United States of America
May 2002
10 9 8 7 6 5 4 3 2 1
First American Edition

To Gwilym and Eleri

Contents

Dad

Dad

The Quigleys lived in the middle of their street, in a house with a red door. There was a mass of rose bushes in the front yard and a smell of cat. The Quigleys didn't have a cat. The smell was made by other people's cats.

Will Quigley was tall and blonde. His sister Lucy was small and chunky. For some reason Mum and Dad hardly ever called her Lucy. They called her Poodle, or sometimes Poodlefish. They didn't call Will anything but Will. No-one could explain this.

The Peacheys lived two doors down in a house without a front fence. Mr Peachey – Ben – had planted a single laurel bush with dusty leaves, which cats avoided, even the

Peacheys' own, Fatbrain. 'Not enough cover,' Ben said smugly. Fatbrain favoured the Quigleys' rose bushes. Ben's children were Will and Lucy's best friends. Their names were Elizabeth, Timothy and Pokehead.

One afternoon there was a knock at the door. Lucy was the first to reach it. She liked answering the door – she was just tall enough to open it, standing on tiptoe on the skirting board and pulling herself up by the handle to reach the latch. She liked opening it a crack and peeping out.

'Hullo,' Ben said, peeping in. 'There's a smell out here.'

'I know,' Lucy said. 'It's cat's poo.'

After a while she let him in. Lucy liked Ben. She liked his fair hair and his glasses. They stood together in the hall.

'Mum's in bed,' Lucy said. 'Mums need rest,' she added.

Ben asked if her dad was in.

Will appeared briefly at the top of the stairs, wearing boxing gloves and carrying a copy of *The Beano*, and drifted away again. Then Dad came out of his study, looking distracted. He often looked distracted. It wasn't just his face that looked distracted, it was his hair and arms and eyebrows too. Even the sleeves of his shirt looked distracted.

He came downstairs and talked to Ben. It seemed that tonight was the night of Ben's office party, and their babysitter had let them down. Dad pulled his ears and looked friendly. When he wanted to, Dad could look very friendly.

'Yes, of course,' he said. 'I'd be happy to.'

When Ben had gone, Lucy said to Dad, 'Are you going to babysit for Elizabeth, Timothy and Pokehead?'

Dad nodded.

'Tonight?'

He nodded again.

'Can I come?'

He shook his head.

'I could help.'

'You couldn't.'

'I could.'

'You couldn't, Poodlefish.'

'I could help with the midnight feast.'

'There won't be a midnight feast.'

'Why won't there be a midnight feast?'
'Because of the football match.'
Lucy looked at him.
'I don't mean football match,' Dad said quickly. 'I mean because of having to go to sleep. Or Timothy won't be able to play in his football match tomorrow.'
Lucy said, 'Are you going to be watching football on the television all evening?'
'Don't be silly,' Dad said. 'I'll be babysitting. Babysitting's a very responsible job.'

When Dad said goodnight to Lucy and Will that evening, he told them he was going round to the Peacheys' house and said that they were not to disturb Mum. 'Mum's very tired,' he said.
Will, in the top bunk, said, 'Are you babysitting?'
Dad nodded.
'Can I come?' Will sat up in bed. 'Timothy's got a new computer game.'
'No.'

Will scowled.

'Dad's going to watch the football,' Lucy said helpfully.

Will scowled so hard the whole of his forehead seemed to fold down over his face.

'Nonsense,' Dad said quickly. 'Anyway, it's not till later.'

'You never let me do what I want,' Will said. 'Never. And *you* do what you want *all* the time.'

'Now, Will.'

'You *never ever* let me do anything I want. You *never ever ever* . . .'

'Stop it, Will, before I get cross. Now, come on. Give me a kiss before I go.'

Will immediately rolled as far away from Dad as it was possible to get, and put his hands over his ears. Dad lifted his face to the ceiling and shouted, 'Just give me a kiss!' And at once there was a cry from upstairs and the sound of coughing, and Mum called out weakly, 'What's going on? Who woke me up?'

Dad left the room, looking distracted.

The Peacheys' house was exactly the same as the Quigleys', but everything was the other way round. It was like looking in a mirror. You turned left, not right, to go into the living room. The stairs went up to the right, not the left, and when you got to the top you turned left, not right, into the bathroom. Even the cord for the bathroom light was hanging on the wrong side of the bathroom door.

'Good,' Dad said, as he finished reading a story to Timothy and Pokehead in the living room. 'Up we go. Elizabeth's already in bed.'

Timothy and Pokehead ignored him.

'Bedtime,' Dad said, glancing at his watch. 'You monsters,' he added.

'I don't go to bed,' Pokehead said conversationally.

'She doesn't,' Timothy said.

'Of course she does,' Dad said. 'We all go to bed. We all need our sleep.'

'I don't,' Pokehead said. She turned her face to him and stared at him unblinkingly. She had a wide face, very smooth skin and deep-set clear eyes. She looked capable of anything.

Dad said, 'Remember what your mum and dad said.'

'They can't do anything with me either,' Pokehead said.

Dad thought for a moment. He looked anxiously at his watch and glanced briefly towards the television set. Then he picked

Pokehead up and tucked her under his arm.
This seemed to surprise her. He carried her
upstairs, and Timothy followed, looking
interested. Taking advantage of the
impression he'd created, Dad brushed their
teeth and made sure they went to the toilet.
He tucked them in, Timothy in the top
bunk, Pokehead in the bottom, and turned
off the light. And turned it on again to look
for Timothy's wet rabbit, which he found in
the toilet, and turned it off again. And
turned it on for the second time to look for
Pokehead's five knitted penguins, which he

found, eventually, already in her bed. And turned off the light for the *last* time, saying that he was *not* turning it on again in *any* circumstances, and said goodnight, and went down the stairs two at a time, looking distracted, and dashed into the  living room, where he immediately turned on the television. He stared at it. Though the game had started only ten minutes earlier, the score was already 2-1, and the commentator was saying that never, in all his life, had he seen such a wonderful opening to a game. Swearing openly because there were no children around, Dad sank into a chair, and when he turned his head he found Pokehead standing next to him.

'What did you say?' she asked, staring at him. Before he could reply, she said, 'Have you fed Fatbrain yet? I'll show you how to do it, if you want. First you have to get a big knife.'

When Pokehead was back in bed, about a minute later, Dad returned to the television and found that the score was now 2-2. The television commentator was choking with excitement. Almost immediately, from upstairs came the sounds of a disturbance, and he slowly backed out of the living room, keeping his eyes on the television until the last possible moment.

When he returned to the living room a quarter of an hour later, after separating Timothy and Pokehead, he found no change to the score in the football match, but both sides had had two men sent off. At once there was a crash in the kitchen, and he sprang up from his chair and ran out of the living room.

Pokehead was balancing on one leg on a chair, trying to open a can of cat food with a carving knife.

'I need another knife,' she said, when she saw Dad. 'This one doesn't work properly.'

Dad took the knife off her. 'Listen to me, Pokehead,' he said in a quiet, strained voice.

'I like you. I like your mum and dad.
You're my daughter's best friend. But if you
don't go to bed and settle down now, I'll
make sure you never see her again, as long
as you live.' Then he picked her up and
carried her upstairs.

The rest of the football match on television
was entirely without incident. Dad sat there
considering his evening. He thought that

enough of it had been ruined already. He took a decision: if Pokehead played up any more he would take no notice of her. See how she liked that. This made him feel much better. He wondered if there was any beer in the Peacheys' fridge. There was.

After this, whenever he heard soft footsteps upstairs, he ignored them. Once or twice there was a pattering down in the hall, but he didn't investigate. Only once did he actually catch sight of Pokehead. He turned in his chair to see her tiptoeing past the living room door. But when he opened his mouth to speak, she held a finger to her lips, and tiptoed away again. He stayed where he was, and at last everything was quiet.

After the football match was over he went to check on the children. Elizabeth, who had her own room, was sleeping neatly on her side. Timothy was sprawled on his top bunk as if he'd just dropped off the ceiling, his duvet bunched round him. But Pokehead's bed was empty.

Dad stared at the bed as if a bed was something he'd never seen before. He frisked the duvet with his hands, then got down on his knees and looked under the bed. He checked the top bunk, to see if she'd crawled in with her brother, but there was just Timothy, with his mouth open. He went round the room, looking into the corners. Then he went round again, looking in the book cupboard, behind the curtains and in all the drawers.

'Pokehead?' he whispered. 'Pokehead?' The room was silent except for Timothy's heavy breathing.

Dad swore, though he knew he shouldn't. He left the room – looking very distracted – and began to search through the house.

In bed just down the street, Lucy was
having one of her dreams about doors. She
dreamed she opened a door and went into
a room, and found another door in front of
her. She opened that door and went into
another room the same as the first, with
another door in it, and she opened that
door, and went into another room the same
as the other two. She was just opening the
next door when Dad woke her up.

'It's me,' he hissed. 'Are you awake?'

'No,' she said sleepily. She yawned. 'You mustn't wake Mum either.'

'That's why I'm waking you,' Dad whispered. She opened her eyes. 'You have to help me,' Dad said. He was shaking Will lying next to her. In the night Will had come down to her bed, as usual. Will was scared of the dark, but Lucy didn't mind, she liked him being with her. It was friendlier with two. When Dad shook him, Will woke up with a loud snort, saying, 'Dunno.'

Dad was telling them both something about Pokehead, but he wasn't making any sense.

Will said, 'What do you mean, lost her?'

'Quickly, get dressed,' Dad said. 'Ben and Philippa will be back in half an hour. You have to help me find her.'

In five minutes they were all standing in the Peacheys' hall. It was very quiet and most of the lights were out. It felt strange, as if they shouldn't be there.

'Are we allowed to whisper?' Lucy whispered.

Dad said, 'Listen to me carefully. She's not in her bed, she's not in Timothy's bed, or Elizabeth's. She's not anywhere. I've checked the whole house, I've even been up to the attic, which she couldn't possibly get to.' He thought about this. 'Which I don't *think* she could have got to. I've checked all the windows, I've looked in the cupboard under the stairs, I've been out in the back garden. Nothing,' he said. 'There are two possibilities. One is that she's had an accident somewhere in the house, somewhere where we can't hear her. Like the roof,' he said grimly. 'The other . . .' He went pale. 'The other possibility is that she left the house.'

'How could she have left the house?' Will said. 'You'd have seen her.'

Dad said nothing.

'Was it when you were watching football on the television?' Lucy asked helpfully.

Dad swallowed. 'I'm going out there now,' he said. 'You two have to stay here in case Timothy or Elizabeth wakes up. Don't wake them deliberately though, they'd only be frightened. Try to think of places Pokehead might be. Little places,' he added. 'Dark, little places where she'd know I'd never find her.'

Then he went. They heard him calling down the street: 'Pokehead! Come home, Pokehead!'

The Peacheys' house was hushed and strange. The rooms were different colours from the Quigleys', and they had different smells, and everything was the wrong way round.

'You have to hold hands, Will,' Lucy said.

Holding hands, they went upstairs. In Pokehead's room, Will climbed up the bunk-bed ladder and looked at Timothy as he slept.

'His mouth's open,' he whispered to Lucy.

Then they stood on the landing, holding hands.

'I don't want to go into the attic,' Lucy said.

'Dad's already looked in the attic.'

'Dad's already looked everywhere. Is Dad in trouble, Will?'

They stood there thinking about Dad.

'I have to go to the toilet,' Lucy said. 'You have to come with me.'

Still holding hands, they went along the landing to the bathroom, and Will found the light switch, though it was on the wrong side of the door. They were very quiet, and they could hear how quiet the house was.

Lucy sat on the toilet, feeling scared.

'I'm scared, Will,' she said. 'I don't want to go and look in those dark, little places. I want to stay here.'

Will said, in a strange voice, 'I've got to go and check the roof.'

Lucy knew Will was frightened of the dark. 'Don't go, Will,' she said. 'You'll be scared.'

'Dad said I had to,' he said. He walked stiffly across the bathroom, holding his arms against his sides, and when he turned to her his face had gone flat the way it did when he was determined.

'He didn't, Will,' Lucy said. 'Don't go. Stay here with me.'

'I have to,' Will said. Lucy noticed that he was standing up very straight. And then he went.

Now Lucy was alone. She sat on the toilet in the Peacheys' bathroom, feeling scared. The house was quieter than ever. She imagined Will creeping out on to the dark roof high above her. She was good at imagining things, making up stories in her head, but she didn't like this story, and when she'd imagined Will climbing up the steep, wet roof and clinging on to the chimney, she wanted to stop. Once, from the street outside, she heard Dad's faint voice: 'Pokehead! Poke-head!' Then it was gone. She couldn't help herself: she gave a few little gasps, and felt the tears come into her eyes.

Then suddenly Will was in the bathroom again, sitting with his back against the wall, and holding his arm, as if he'd hurt it.

'Will!' she cried. 'Did you find her?'

Will said nothing, nursing his arm, and panting slightly.

'Have you hurt yourself, Will? Did you go right over the roof?'

'I've got to talk to Dad,' Will said gruffly.

'You were very brave, Will,' Lucy said.

Will began to soften. He gave an enormous wince and said, 'It's nothing, just a scratch. I didn't go *all* the way over the roof. You can't get *all* the way over. Actually,' he said, 'you can't get onto the roof at all, not from the house. But there's a window in Ben and Philippa's room, really high up, and, if you hold on right, you can lean out and look onto the roof. Onto a bit of the roof anyway.'

Lucy looked at him with admiration. 'Did you lean out, Will?' she asked.

He shrugged. 'I could have done,' he said, 'if I'd had to.' He was going to say more, but they heard Dad come in the front door, and they ran together to the top of the stairs. He was alone.

'Are you two all right?' he called, looking up.

'She's not on the roof, Dad,' Will said in the gruff voice he'd used before.

Dad looked at him in a funny way. Then he said, 'Thanks, Will. I knew I could count on you.'

'What are you going to do now, Dad?' Will asked.

'I'm going to call the police,' he said.

Lucy and Will stayed at the top of the stairs, and listened to him talking on the phone. 'Six years old,' they heard him say. 'About an hour ago.' Then he came out of the living room, and said to them, 'They're on their way. Ben and Philippa will be here soon, as well. From wherever it is they've gone.'

'Ben's office party,' said Lucy, who was good at remembering things about people.

'Yes, the office party,' Dad said. 'Do you two want to go back home now?'

Lucy shook her head. Will said, 'We want to stay with you, Dad.'

Lucy and Will sat on the top step, while Dad paced up and down the hallway below.

'He is in trouble, isn't he, Will?' Lucy whispered, but Will didn't say anything.

Lucy wished she could do something to help. Dad had been searching the streets, and Will had been up on the roof – well, almost – but Lucy had been too scared to do anything. She found herself thinking about Pokehead instead, trying to imagine what she'd been doing that evening, before she disappeared. Lucy began to make up a story in her head about Pokehead being babysat by Dad.

In her story, Dad told Pokehead to go to bed but she didn't want to, so she played by herself round the house, little games she made up on her own, quiet, creeping games because she didn't want Dad to catch her. Anyway, Dad was watching television. Pokehead played going out to the shops, and going visiting, and being a princess telling all her tiny people what to do. But Timothy and Elizabeth were already asleep, so there was no-one to play with, and as she played and played, she got

tireder and tireder.

When Lucy had thought all these things, the police arrived. She could see the blue light on top of their car flashing through the glass panes in the front door. Dad went out and talked to them on the front path, and Will went downstairs so he could hear what they were saying.

Lucy went back to her story. If she was Pokehead playing by herself in the quiet house, and getting tireder and tireder, she wouldn't have gone outside, not even if

Dad was busy watching television. She would have curled up somewhere warm to go to sleep. Where would she have gone? She'd have gone to bed. But her own bed wouldn't have been as warm and friendly as Timothy's or Elizabeth's.

Lucy went into Pokehead's room, trying to imagine being Pokehead feeling sleepy, and climbed up the bunk-bed ladder. Timothy was asleep on his back, and the duvet was bunched round him, and Lucy could see at once that there was no-one in bed with him. She stood there looking at Timothy, thinking that if she was Pokehead she'd crawl in, and burrow and snuggle up with him, to get warm, now that she'd stopped playing by herself in the cool, quiet house.

As she stood there on the ladder, she heard other voices downstairs. Ben and Philippa were back from their party, and Ben was saying, 'What sort of problem exactly?'

As she was listening to the voices, she

saw Timothy make a funny movement in bed. It was funny because he moved and didn't move at the same time. She looked hard. Timothy was very still, lying on his back and not moving at all, just breathing heavily with his mouth open. But the duvet was moving round him. Lucy put out her hand and felt it, and it wasn't soft and flat, but hard and lumpy and hot. Suddenly the duvet gave a sigh. As quickly as she could, she undid some of the poppers, and inside the duvet cover was Pokehead, fast asleep.

Lucy was so excited she nearly fell off the ladder. She scrambled down, and ran across the landing. She could hear Ben and the

policeman and Dad all talking below, and she knew she shouldn't interrupt, but she stood at the top of the stairs and shouted, 'I've found her! I've found Pokehead, and she's fast asleep inside the duvet cover, where she crept to get warm when she stopped playing in the cold house, and did up the poppers again, because it's always friendlier with two!'

When the Quigleys got home it was midnight, but Mum had woken up, and they all got into Mum and Dad's bed, and had hot chocolate, and Dad and Will and Lucy told her about Pokehead. Dad said that Will was as brave as a lion for going up to look on the roof, and that Lucy was the cleverest girl in the world for knowing where Pokehead was.

'But how did you know?' Mum said, and Lucy told her about pretending to be Pokehead, and about how it was always friendlier in bed with two, but she was so tired she couldn't keep awake, and she kept

33

yawning, and forgetting what she was saying.

'Will's asleep,' Dad said.

'I think Lucy is too,' Mum said.

'No, I'm not,' Lucy said, but she wasn't sure if she said it out loud or just in her head, she was so tired. But she heard Mum say, 'I think they can stay here tonight.' And she heard Dad say, 'If it's friendlier with two, think how friendly it is with four.'

And ten minutes later all the Quigleys were asleep in Mum and Dad's bed.

Lucy

Lucy

The Quigleys were invited to a wedding,
and Lucy was asked to be bridesmaid.

'Bridesmaid!' Dad said. 'Just think of
that, Poodle. Being a bridesmaid is an
extremely important job.'

'I know that,' Lucy said. Lucy was a
good girl, but she hated being told what to
do, and sometimes she was stubborn. All the
Quigleys could be a little stubborn.

'You'll have a special dress to wear, and
ribbons for your hair, and probably a
bouquet of flowers to carry.'

'Yes, I know,' Lucy said impatiently.

'And you'll have to walk down the aisle
behind the bride, and be her special helper,
and do all the things she asks you to do.'

'I *know* all that,' Lucy said. 'Stop going

on!' She was quite angry, and she ran upstairs, to teach Dad a lesson.

Later in the week Mum and Lucy met Madeleine, the bride-to-be, to discuss the bridesmaids' outfits. Madeleine was one of Mum's best friends. She had red hair, which she dyed herself, and her house was all yellow and green. Lucy liked Madeleine's hair, and she liked her house, but she didn't like her bridesmaids' dresses.

While Lucy sat there, Mum and Madeleine talked about the dresses, and Madeleine showed Mum lots of pictures and patterns. The dresses were going to be navy blue taffeta, with puff sleeves, and a sea green sash round the middle, and a stiff net petticoat, and there were going to be matching ribbons for the hair, and little baskets of flowers to carry.

'It sounds gorgeous,' Mum said. 'Doesn't it, Lucy?'

Lucy shook her head.

Mum gave Lucy a warning look. Madeleine, who didn't have children of her

own, and wasn't as firm as she should be, said, 'What do *you* want, Lucy?'

Lucy thought for a moment. 'I want to be a bee,' she said.

They looked at her.

'A bee?'

'A bee, with yellow and black stripes, and wings, and wagglers on its head.'

Madeleine began to laugh, and Mum said quickly, 'Not at the wedding, Poodle. Not in the *church*.'

Lucy nodded.

'Not *really*,' Mum said soothingly. 'We can make you a bee costume for another time.'

Lucy shook her head.

Madeleine laughed again, and said that Lucy could be a bee if she really wanted to, and Mum said firmly, 'Of course not, Lucy really wants to wear the gorgeous blue dress *in church*, don't you, Poodle?' She gave her another warning look, and Lucy shook her head furiously, because they'd laughed at her, and then they went home.

For quite a while after this, Mum didn't mention the bridesmaid's dress. But one Saturday morning at the beginning of September, she asked Lucy to go into town with her to buy some material.

'What material?' Lucy asked.

'Well,' Mum said. 'For the bridesmaid's dress.'

Lucy ran upstairs, and Mum followed her. After ten minutes or so, she came down and sent Dad up. Ten minutes later, he came down.

'She wants to be a bee,' he said.

'I know *that*,' Mum said. 'But she *can't* be a bee. It's not that sort of wedding, it's going to be very smart. And Madeleine's paying for all the material.'

'Oh,' Dad said.

'Think of the photographs,' Mum said. 'You'll have to talk to Lucy. Talk her out of the bee thing.'

Dad looked distracted. 'I'll try,' he said.

Later in the morning, Dad and Lucy went to the park to feed the ducks.

'About this bee thing,' Dad began casually, and Lucy immediately ran to the furthest side of the boating pond, where she stayed until Dad shouted to her that he wouldn't talk about it again.

Then they went to the lake to throw in their bread.

'Don't eat it, Poodle,' Dad said.

There were mallards, swans, moorhens, coots and grebes on the water; the grebes stayed shyly in the middle of the lake, keeping their distance, but the other birds came towards them straightaway.

'At least don't eat the blue bits,' Dad said to Lucy, after a while.

As they were feeding the ducks, an elderly lady came along the path with a child the same age as Lucy. When she saw Dad, she waved and made her way towards them.

Dad waved back. 'Lucy, who's this?' he said out of the corner of his mouth. Dad had an embarrassing problem with people's names: he couldn't remember them. He couldn't even remember the names of people he knew well. And when he forgot the name of someone whose name he really ought to know, because for instance they were one of his best friends, he panicked. Whenever he could, he turned to Lucy for help, because she remembered everything about people.

'Quick,' he whispered. 'Before she gets here.'

'Ruth,' Lucy said. 'You know Ruth, Dad. She's Madeleine's mum. You remember, who's getting married.'

Smiling and gently waving at Ruth, Dad spoke in a fast, squashed voice: 'Ruth, of course, yes. And her granddaughter, what's her name?'

'Lottie.'

'Lottie, yes, yes. Isn't there someone else?'

'Sandy, her brother.'

'Sandy. Good. And what about their mother? Quickly, Poodle.'

'Sophie, Dad. Madeleine's sister.'

By this time Ruth had almost reached them, and Dad called out in his friendliest voice, 'Ruth, how are you? How's Lottie? Sandy not with you today? Sophie's working, I suppose.'

Lucy played shops with Lottie behind an ornamental stone, while Dad talked to Ruth, and after they went, Dad said to her, 'Thanks, Poodle. You saved me. I really rely on you. You're a very good girl.' He gave her a big hug, and then he said, 'Now, about the bee thing . . .' And Lucy ran home ahead of him, and wouldn't speak to him for ages and ages, to make sure he knew he'd done something very wrong.

Mum asked Dad if he'd talked Lucy into the bridesmaid's dress, and Dad said he'd certainly made a start.

'We've got two months,' Mum said. 'She can be stubborn, but she can't be stubborn for two months, can she?'

Mum thought it best if she made the bridesmaid's dress without Lucy's help. But one afternoon, Lucy saw Mum cutting out the taffeta on the floor in the front room.

'What's that?' she asked.

'It's a special dress,' Mum said. 'Do you like it?'

Lucy looked at it for a while. 'It doesn't look special to me,' she said. 'It looks like that horrid bridesmaid's dress.'

Mum tried treats. She said that if Lucy would wear the navy blue bridesmaid's dress at Madeleine's wedding, she'd buy her a pair of roller skates, and Lucy said she hated roller skating. Mum said she'd take her to the café at the Museum of Modern Art for hot chocolate, and Lucy said she hated hot chocolate, which she didn't.

'Well, what *do* you want then?' Mum said.

Lucy said she wanted to be a bee.

After this, Mum tried threats. She said that if Lucy didn't wear the navy blue taffeta bridesmaid's dress at Madeleine's wedding, she couldn't expect to be taken to a Christmas show. Lucy just scowled.

'And I don't even know if I can buy you a lovely bee costume *after* the wedding,' Mum said.

Lucy scowled so hard she couldn't see.

'Don't do that,' Mum said. 'You look like Will.'

46

So Lucy ran upstairs instead, and squeezed into the space between her bed and the wall, and covered herself with a blanket from her doll's pram, which is what she always did when she was very  upset. It comforted her, she didn't know why. It was a bit like disappearing.

Downstairs Mum was talking to Dad. Lucy heard Mum say, 'Thank God she doesn't actually have a bee costume.'

After a while, Lucy wriggled out of her hiding place, and went over to the bottom shelf in Will's wardrobe, where they kept the dressing-up clothes, and began to search through it.

When Dad came up later, she was sitting on a pile of clothes, trying to cut up one of Mum's old jumpers with a pair of plastic stationery scissors.

'You won't get far with those, Poodle,'

Dad said. 'They're for cutting paper. I'll get you a proper pair from Mum's sewing box.'

He came back with a large pair of shears which Mum had said Lucy should never ever use. 'Be careful with them,' he said. 'What are you making?'

'Nothing,' she said.

Over the next few days, Mum and Dad got used to finding Lucy with the dressing-up clothes, cutting them up or trying to stick them together. Sticking them together was especially difficult. Sellotape didn't work very well, nor did Blu-tack or the white glue from the toy cupboard. The flour and water paste which they used for papier maché models didn't work at all. In the end, Lucy asked Mum to teach her how to sew. She learned how to pin the material together, and anchor the thread securely, and push the needle through and pull it out the other side, weaving it in and out, in and out. 'Like a fish with a tail,' she said to Mum.

After that she was very busy. When she wasn't sewing, she was hunting round the house, asking Mum for odds and ends of things: pipe cleaners, rolls of crêpe paper ('It has to be yellow'), conkers, elastic and chopsticks.

At about the same time, Mum discovered that Lucy had stopped being difficult about the bridesmaid's dress. She still didn't like it, but she was prepared to answer simple questions, such as 'Do you want the sash to have a bow at the back or not?' ('Not') or 'What colour buttons do you want, navy blue or sea green?' ('Sea green').

'I think she's finally coming round,' Mum said to Dad.

Every few days, when she was sure no-one would disturb her, Lucy got out the things she'd made and tried them on. She was very pleased with them. But there were still some things she hadn't been able to make. And for these she knew she needed to think harder.

The next day Lucy came in from the park, limping.

'My wellingtons are too small,' she said.

Dad felt them. 'I think there's still a bit of room in them, Poodle,' he said.

'No,' Lucy said firmly. 'They hurt. You told me to tell you if my shoes start to hurt, and now I'm telling you, and you're not even listening to me.'

'OK, OK,' Dad said. 'We'll get you a new pair of wellingtons. We've got to go to town today anyway.'

The first shop they went into had Barbie wellingtons, Winnie-the-Pooh wellingtons, dinosaur wellingtons and Aladdin wellingtons. Lucy said she didn't like any of them. The second shop had glow-in-the-dark wellingtons, sparkly wellingtons and wellingtons shaped like frogs.

'No,' Lucy said.

They tried three more shops, and Lucy hated the wellingtons in all of them. It wasn't until they got to the last shoe shop in town that she saw what she wanted.

'But these are just ordinary wellingtons,' Mum said. 'We've seen dozens of wellingtons just like them already.'

'Not yellow ones,' Lucy said.

'It doesn't matter what colour wellingtons are,' Dad said.

Lucy said, 'Oh, but it does.'

It was getting close to the day of
Madeleine's wedding, and the navy blue
taffeta bridesmaid's dress was ready. Lucy
agreed to try it on in the front room.

'Hold still while I put the ribbons in,'
Mum said.

Lucy held still, saying nothing. Mum put
the ribbons in.

'Now the sash,' she said.

Lucy held still while Mum tied the sash at
the back.

'Now take this,' Dad said, handing her the little basket that the flowers would go in.

Lucy took the basket, saying nothing.

'Stand like this,' Dad said.

She stood like that, and he gave a happy little sigh.

'Good,' Mum said.

'Perfect, Poodlefish,' Dad said.

Dad gave Mum a kiss, turned and began to say, 'I'm so pleased you're going to wear the . . .'

But the Poodlefish had gone. She had taken off the dress, and was already running upstairs in her vest and navy blue tights.

There was still one thing that Lucy hadn't been able to make. It was too difficult. But if she didn't have it, her whole plan wouldn't work. She didn't know what to do, and she was sitting in the middle of her bedroom floor thinking about it when Dad came in one evening to borrow some money.

'I'll pay you back tomorrow,' he said, taking her piggy bank off the shelf.

Lucy liked lending money to Mum and Dad. They were always so pleased to get it.

'Why are you always borrowing money, Dad?'

'Well, Poodle, I'll tell you. Pubs don't accept cards.'

'Why are you always going to pubs?'

Dad didn't seem to hear that. He rattled the piggy bank. 'I'm not sure there's much in here,' he said. He shook out the coins and counted twenty-five pence, and frowned, and explored the piggy bank more deeply with his fingers.

'Wait a second,' he said. 'I think there's a note. Saved!'

There was, but it wasn't a bank note, it was a crumpled-up piece of paper with a message written on it.

'Oh,' he said sadly. He read the note. It said, '*IOU eight pounds, love Mum.*'

'She got here before me,' Dad said. 'Eight pounds. I didn't know you had so

much money, Poodle. Are you saving up for something?'

Lucy started to shake her head, then stopped. She began to smile.

Dad didn't notice. 'Anyway,' he said thoughtfully. 'Can I take the twenty-five pence?'

When he'd gone, Lucy said to Will, 'Will, if I give you the money, will you buy something for me when you go into town with Dad to buy your new football boots?'

Will looked up from his *Beano* and made a noise like a parrot, and Lucy began to explain again what she wanted him to do.

The morning of Madeleine's wedding was beautiful: clear and cool and blue. Mum and Dad and Will and Lucy were getting ready. They were running late. The

Quigleys were always running late.

'We're late!' Dad shouted. Soon he would be breaking the family rules.

'Can I wear my new football boots?' Will shouted from his room.

'It's a wedding, Will,' Dad shouted from the bathroom. 'Not the first round of the FA Cup.'

Will put on his crinkly blue shirt and his patterned waistcoat and his navy trousers with turn-ups. 'Will this do?' he asked.

Dad appeared on the landing, his chin covered in shaving foam. 'Just take off your goalkeeper gloves,' he said. 'Poodle?' he shouted. 'Are you nearly ready?'

'Nearly,' Lucy shouted from the spare room. 'Don't come in yet.'

Ten minutes later, Dad, Mum and Will were waiting by the front door.

'Lucy!' Dad shouted. 'You've got to come *now*!'

As he spoke, she appeared at the top of the stairs. Dad made a gurgling noise, and then there was silence.

Lucy was dressed as a bee.

She was wearing Mum's old black jumper with yellow crêpe paper stuck in hoops all the way round. On her legs were black tights. On her feet were her new yellow wellingtons. On her head, stuck into her black Alice band, were two pipe cleaners with conkers on top painted black. When she turned round, she showed a long chopstick-sting on elastic round her waist, and, above her shoulders, a pair of enormous gold-framed, sparkly, gauzy wings.

'Christ Almighty!' Dad said, and nobody told him off. 'Where did you get all that from?'

'I made it,' Lucy said.

'I got the wings,' Will said.

They all stared at her, mesmerized.

'It's beautiful,' Mum said. For a moment she just looked at Lucy, and Lucy thought it was all going to be all right. Then Mum seemed to give herself a shake. 'But you can't wear it,' she said. 'You'll have to get changed.'

Mum looked at Dad. Dad looked at his watch. 'No time,' he said.

Lucy smiled.

Mum went into action. 'Then we'll take the bridesmaid's dress with us. She can change when we get there. We should just be able to make it.'

Lucy was still crying when they arrived at the church.

Dad turned round in his seat and said, 'We love your bee costume, Poodle. As soon as the wedding's over, you can put it back on, I promise.'

They left the car and ran to the church.

Mum was one of the ushers, so she had to stand at the church door telling people which side of the church to sit in.

'Over to you,' she said to Dad.

'But,' Dad said.

'There's a vestibule round the side,' Mum said. 'She can change there.' Mum looked at her watch. 'You've got five minutes.'

In the vestibule, Lucy was still crying. Will was holding her hand, even though she hadn't asked him to.

'Come on, Poodle,' Dad said. 'As soon as the wedding's over you can be a bee again.'

He began to undress her. 'I must say, this is really something,' he said, as he struggled with the wings. 'What did you do, weld them on?'

Lucy hardly heard him. She could feel the tears running down her cheeks and dripping onto her shiny yellow wellingtons. She wished she was in her room at home and could squeeze into the space between the bed and the wall, and pull the doll's blanket over her head until she disappeared. She

couldn't disappear in
the church vestibule.
Instead she had to
stand there while Dad
took off her wings.
She thought that she'd
never wanted
anything so much as
to wear her bee
costume at the
wedding. She was so
full of unhappy

thoughts, she didn't hear Dad give a sudden
moan.

'Oh God!' he said. 'It's her!'

Lucy looked up, and saw Madeleine's
mother, Ruth, coming down the path
towards the vestibule. She had both Lottie
and Sandy with her, and she was smiling at
Dad.

Dad ground his teeth. He went to pieces.
'I can't remember their names,' he said. He
looked at Lucy.

Lucy shook her head.

'Please, Poodle,' he whispered.

She shook her head again.

'Will!' Dad whispered hoarsely. 'Quick! What are their names?'

Will looked up from his *Beano*, across at Ruth and back to Dad. 'Dunno,' he said. He was his father's son.

Dad's neck seemed to bulge.

'Poodle,' he begged. 'Poodlefish, why won't you tell me?'

'I want to be a bee,' she said.

Dad was trapped. He saw he was trapped and gave another moan. Ruth, smiling at him through the glass pane of the door, had her hand on the doorhandle.

'All right,' Dad whispered. 'All right.'

'Sandy, Lottie, Ruth,' Lucy whispered.

'Thank God!' Dad exclaimed. He leaped forward to open the door for Ruth.

'Lottie,' he said to her with great warmth. 'How are you on this big day?'

The organ was beginning to play the wedding march as Dad slipped into the seat beside Mum.

'Everything OK?' she asked.

Dad looked straight ahead of him, saying nothing. She noticed he was trembling slightly.

'Is it?' she asked.

Without turning his head, he said in a low, deep voice, 'I've done a terrible thing.'

Before he could say any more, the organ music swelled to a crescendo and everyone turned to look at the bride. Or not, actually, at the bride. At the bridesmaids. Or not, actually, at the bridesmaids, but at one bridesmaid in particular. A bubbling noise of surprised excitement spread through the congregation, followed by a warm

murmur of appreciation. Everyone was craning their necks to get a good view, people were pointing and smiling, and some were even applauding.

Mum said to Dad, 'I don't think I can look. Just tell me if Madeleine's smiling.'

At that moment, Madeleine came past in her white dress, and Dad said, 'Look now.' And as Mum turned, Madeleine broke off smiling just long enough to mouth the words, 'I love it!'

She went past, and behind her came the bridesmaids, three navy blue taffeta bridesmaids and one bee, pink-faced, a little trembly and very pleased.

For months afterwards it was the habit at Quigley family occasions to bring out the wedding photographs. There was the one of the bee sniffing a large paper rose. There was the one of the navy blue taffeta bridesmaids standing round the bee, admiring its stripes and wings and wagglers. And there was the one of the bride giving the bee an enormous smiley hug. The photographs would come out so often, and people would say the same things so often, that the bee herself would sometimes get a bit bored.

'I love the stripes best,' Mum would say, and the bee would say, 'I know. You told me before.'

'I love the wagglers,' Dad would say, and the bee would say, 'Yes, I know that already.'

'I like the wings,' Will would say. 'Didn't I buy those?' And the bee would say, 'I know all that! Stop going on!'

Mum

Mum

On the morning of Mum's birthday, the day she was going to the ballet with Dad, she made Will and Lucy get up earlier than usual because Will was going on a school trip and had to dress as a Saxon. His cloak, jerkin, belt and leg-thongs were laid out on the floor ready.

Will and Lucy hated getting up, even at the normal time. All the Quigleys hated getting up. Their moods were not good first thing in the morning. But today of all days, Mum was determined to be calm and sweet and good-natured.

She gave both of them a tiny little shake.

'Time to get up,' she said sweetly. Will woke up but didn't move. Lucy didn't wake at all. 'We have to be extra quick this

69

morning,' Mum said brightly.

Lying clenched under the duvet with his eyes screwed shut, Will knew at once it was going to be an awful day.

'All right,' he heard Mum say eventually. 'Five minutes to come to.'

This did not alter Will's mood. Five minutes was *nothing*. Anyway, he knew that she wouldn't actually wait five minutes. Practically straightaway, it seemed, just as he was going back to sleep, she went into action again, pulling off his duvet before he could grab it, and *talking*. Rearing up suddenly in front of her, he cried in a terrible voice, 'What's the time?'

'Nearly seven o'clock, Will,' Mum said when she had recovered, and, as if struck on the head, he fell back at once and rolled onto his side and immediately began to breathe deeply. Sometimes, if he concentrated hard on the darkness behind his eyelids, he could make himself fall asleep. It felt like pitching forward slowly into something soft. If he breathed slower and slower, he would start to topple forward into the darkness, and he would sort of melt into the bed. But just as he was melting, Mum gave him another shake, and he gave a hopeless groan and realized crossly that he was awake.

'Now you, Lucy,' Mum said.

Lucy's eyes were gummed together. She kept them tight shut, and clung like a monkey to her duvet as Mum tried to pull it away. With the duvet half off, it was as cold in the bedroom as it was outside, and the brightness of the electric light hurt her eyes, even though they were still tightly shut.

They struggled for a moment, then the rest of the duvet came away.

'Come on, Poodle,' Mum said in a sympathetic voice. 'You have to get dressed now. Tell me what you want to wear.'

'Bed,' Lucy shouted.

Eventually she got up and started dressing. It was awful. The legs of her knickers jumbled themselves together, and the armholes of her vest vanished, and none of the buttons worked, and her shoes hurt.

'I feel sick,' she whispered as she groped for the sleeve of her cardigan.

'Never mind,' Mum said. 'You'll feel better when you open your eyes.'

'These leg-thongs are the wrong *sort* of leg-thongs,' Will was saying. Taking off the leg-thongs, he asked what the point was.

Mum patiently explained the point. 'But I am starting to get a teeny bit annoyed,' she said.

'And why *can't* I take my spear?' Will said, ignoring her. '*Everyone* else will have weapons. You *never* let me have weapons,

and everyone else always has *all sorts* of
weapons.'

Mum somehow stopped herself shouting.
Closing her mouth, she turned round and
quietly left the room. Her lips, Will and
Lucy noticed, were tightly shut as if her
mouth was full of something unpleasant.

Will sat on the floor, still scowling at his
leg-thongs, and Lucy sat on the bed, still
scowling at him, and both of them felt that
it was terrible to have to wake up at all, let
alone wake up *earlier than usual*. For a

moment they wondered if perhaps, just maybe, they were being unfair on Mum. But neither of them moved until they heard her coming back up the stairs, when they jumped up and finished getting dressed in a great rush, and stood there with their shoes undone and their hair unbrushed, scowling and waiting to see what Mum would do.

Mum stood in the doorway breathing deeply. She smiled a smile which wasn't a smile. Will and Lucy knew what it was. It was a sort of warning, and they felt cross and upset all over again.

'Today of all days,' Mum said quietly, 'I am determined to be calm and sweet and good-natured.'

But she said it so quietly, Will had to shout, 'What?'

She repeated it. 'It isn't going to be an awful day,' she said in the same calm, quiet voice, 'because we're all going to be calm and sweet and good-natured.'

'Calm?' Will said in disgust.

'Yes, calm.'

She came into the room with that calm smile. 'So take your football boots off, Will,' she said pleasantly. 'The Anglo-Saxons didn't wear them.'

She brushed Lucy's hair and Lucy yelled, and Mum said, very calmly, 'The thing is, Lucy, you really shouldn't chew your hair.'

'It's nothing to do with chewing!' Lucy yelled. 'It's to do with *pain!*'

And Mum said calmly, but with feeling, 'I do *hope* we're all going to be calm and sweet and good-natured.'

Eventually they went down for breakfast. There was no Red Berry Special K, and Mum had to explain four times that they couldn't have chocolate spread on their toast because it wasn't the weekend, which was one of the stupider family rules, and in the end they all ate cornflakes in silence.

'I think things are going to get much better now,' Mum said as they left the house.

But at the end of the road, Will walked backwards into a brick wall for reasons which he couldn't afterwards explain, and going through the park, Lucy soaked the same foot in two separate puddles, and in the end they were late, and, though it seemed incredible, everyone was cross with them for being late and wet and in pain.

These were some of the reasons why their morning was so awful, despite the calm.

Their day at school was awful for different reasons. On Will's trip, no-one was armed except Timothy, and Mr Sheringham took his weapon off him because, he said, the Anglo-Saxons had not invented the automatic pistol. Later, during the copper-beating session, Will hammered his thumb and the nail went purple. At lunchtime he discovered that rain had got into his lunch-box, and all his sandwiches were wet and tasted of washing-up water.

Back at Parkside, Lucy got her sums wrong and was spoken to in what she called a 'dark green' voice by Miss Putz. She hated her lunch, which was cool stew with a skin on and 'scab pudding' for afters, and, to make things worse, it rained all afternoon so they had to stay in the classroom at break, with all the windows steamed up, and everyone in a bad temper.

At last school ended.

Lucy and Will waited for Mum by the gates.

'I think today has to get better now, Will,' Lucy said. 'Don't you think so?'

'I bet that's just what she'll say,' Will said in disgust. 'You just watch. She'll say that it's a good day after all, you just watch her. She hasn't had her thumb hammered flat.'

Mum arrived at four o'clock, half an hour late, having been delayed in heavy traffic on the ring road.

'Did you have a good day?' she asked. Her voice was bright, but there was something wrong with her face. It was a funny pale colour.

'It was a rotten day,' Will said. 'And you promised it wouldn't be.'

Mum said she was sorry. She said, rather quietly, that she hadn't had a very good day herself.

'Absolutely rotten, as I knew it would be,' Will said, and Lucy burst into tears because she'd just remembered how terrible the stew and scab pudding had been.

After they had finished tea, Mum lay on the settee in the front room, which she didn't usually do. She didn't do anything, she just lay there in silence. There were creases in her forehead, and her face was that funny pale colour.

Will and Lucy looked at her for a while, and when she didn't open her eyes they had an argument. Mum kept her eyes closed. The creases in her forehead got deeper, but she didn't open her eyes even when they started shouting.

'It's mine, Will,' Lucy said.

'No, it's not, it's mine,' Will said.

'Isn't!'

'Get off, Lucy!'

'You have to give it back!'

'Get *off*, Lucy!'

Something overturned. There was a crash and Lucy began to scream.

'Now you've really done it, *Lucy*,' Will shouted.

Mum finally opened her eyes, and was cross, despite what she'd promised.

'Give it to me,' she said in a quiet, cross voice. 'Give me whatever you're arguing about.'

Scowling, Will handed it to her.

She held it in the palm of her hand.

'Is this it?'

She held up a small, slightly soft red lump of something, about the size of a marble.

Will was scowling so hard he couldn't talk, but Lucy shouted, 'It's mine! It's mine! You promised, Will!'

'What is it?' Mum said, looking at the small red lump.

There was a short silence while the children considered this unimportant question.

'From the cheese,' Will said shortly.

'What?'

'It was round the cheese.'

'This is what the argument was about?' Mum said. 'The wax from round the Edam at teatime?'

'It's mine,' Lucy wailed.

This would be the moment when Mum usually shouted, but she seemed too pale to shout, and anyway the telephone suddenly rang. Lucy answered it. It was Dad, phoning from a train. Lucy talked to him for a while.

'I'm fine,' she said in the cheerful voice she always used on the phone. 'Yes, she's fine too. We had Damn for tea. No, it's a cheese. Yes, it was nice.'

Then she gave the phone to Mum.

The children listened to her.

'Yes?' Mum said into the receiver. She did not use a cheerful voice.

Then she said, 'Oh.'

And then, '*How* late?'

And finally, in an even quieter voice, 'I'd rather not go at all than go on my own.'

When she put the phone down, Lucy said she was still hungry, and Mum said she could make herself a sandwich, and her voice was so quiet Lucy could hardly hear her.

Lucy made her favourite sandwich, which was peanut butter and pickle, and gave half to Will, and made another, even bigger sandwich, which neither of them wanted, and when they came out of the kitchen Mum had disappeared.

They shouted for her for a while but there was no answer.

'She's gone to Philippa's,' Will said. 'Typical. This really is an awful day.' But he said it unenthusiastically because he was so tired. He began to read *The Beano*.

'She was angry, wasn't she?' Lucy said. 'She was angry with us.'

Will didn't say anything. The house seemed very quiet without Mum. It was incredible to think how much noise she must make when she was there.

'Why is she at Philippa's, Will?' Lucy asked after a while. Will shrugged.

'When's she coming back?' she asked.

'Dunno,' he said.

It was very quiet in the house.

'It was an awful day, wasn't it, Will?' she said.

Will didn't say anything. He had the

feeling that it was time to stop saying how awful the day had been. He stared at his *Beano* without reading it.

'I think we should sit near the front door,' Lucy said, and they went and sat in the hallway. They held hands even though neither of them had said anything about needing to, and listened to the noises outside, a car going past with a *shush*, footsteps ticking on the pavement, a far-off siren like Will's clarinet when he made a mistake.

Still Mum didn't come back, and the house was very quiet.

'Suppose she hasn't gone to Philippa's?' Lucy whispered. 'Suppose she's gone somewhere else?'

'Like where?'

'I don't know. Just somewhere else.'

Lucy felt sad. She had a picture in her mind of Mum going down the street in her blue wool coat, looking tired.

'I don't think we were very nice to Mum,' she said softly.

Will fidgeted with *The Beano*.

In the end, they decided to give themselves a bath and went upstairs, and as soon as they reached the landing, they heard it.

'Listen!' Lucy said. From Mum and Dad's room in the attic, they heard a noise.

Will frowned. 'It sounds like that thing they use at school for getting rid of the vegetable peelings.'

'Somebody's snoring,' Lucy said excitedly.

They ran up the stairs to the attic and

stood in the darkened room. Even in the
dark, they could see the shape of Mum
lying in bed, and could hear her breathing.

'She's asleep, Will,' Lucy whispered.

'I know,' Will said.

'She must be very tired,' Lucy said. 'Poor
Mum.'

'I don't suppose we have to have a bath

now,' Will said.

'I want a bath,' Lucy said.

'So do I,' said Will, after a moment.

They sat in the bath talking.

'It's not fair,' Lucy said.

'I know,' Will said, half-heartedly starting
to scowl again. 'It's been an awful, awful
day.'

'No, I mean it's not fair *on Mum*.'

'Oh,' Will said. 'Why?' he added.

'Because it's her birthday.'

He looked surprised. 'Are you sure?'

'Yes. Dad said. And she can't go to the ballet.'

Will looked at her suspiciously. 'What ballet?'

'The ballet she was going to for her birthday treat. She can't go because Dad's train's broken down. That's what he told me on the telephone.'

'Oh.'

'So it's not fair on Mum.'

'You said that before,' Will said.

'So what shall we do, Will?'

There was a longish pause.

'Think of something, Will,' Lucy said.

'We could make her something to eat,' he said at last. 'She likes toast. And we could put chocolate spread on it for her.'

'That's good. What else, Will?'

He screwed his face up and thought a bit more. 'We could blow up some balloons.'

'That's very good. What else, Will?'

'Hang on a minute,' he said. 'I can't keep thinking of things all the time, one after the other, just like that. You have to give me time.'

He frowned massively and jutted out his chin, while Lucy waited, gazing at him.

'We can give her a glass of wine,' he said at last.

'That's a very good idea indeed,' Lucy said. 'Wine. And sherry.'

'And other things like that,' Will said.

'Wine and sherry and beer and that stuff in the green bottle with ice. She likes all that. She's always drinking them. We can give her all of them, because it's her birthday.'

In the kitchen, they found quite a lot of things in the freezer that you didn't really have to cook, and lots of different sorts of drinks, including some they hadn't seen before at the back of the cupboard where the baking things were kept, and they poured them all out, and mixed some of them, to make pretty birthday colours, and put the glasses on the tray.

'I know what,' Lucy said suddenly. 'We can do a show as well.'

'What show?' Will became suspicious again.

'A ballet show.'

Will looked doubtful.

'Yes, we can, Will. Because Mum was going to a ballet show, and now she can't, so we can dress up and just before we give her the tea we can do dancing and sing something, and you can be the prince if you

want to. Do you want to be the prince,
Will?'

'I'd rather be a wolf,' he said. 'I mean, if
I've got to be something. Is there a wolf?'

'Yes, there's a wolf,' Lucy said.

'OK then,' he said.

For a little time they practised in their
bedroom with the tape recorder. Will
wasn't as keen as Lucy, so she was very
encouraging.

'Good,' she kept saying. 'Good, Will. But when you do your dance you have to put *The Beano* down.'

At last Lucy decided they were ready, and they got the tray of Mum's tea, and tiptoed up to the attic with it, which was quite difficult because they had the tape recorder as well, and their costumes kept tripping them up, but eventually they got there with most of the things still on the tray.

Then Lucy said, 'Are you ready, Will?' And when he didn't say anything, because as soon as he'd put the tray down he'd picked up *The Beano*, she said, 'You have to say "yes", Will.'

'Yes,' he said.

And then they switched on the light and went in.

It was nine o'clock when Dad got home, two hours late and soaked through. He had a wet bunch of roses in his hand. He'd been stuck on the London train. It had been an awful day.

He expected to find the children quietly sleeping in their room, and Mum quietly crying downstairs. But there was no-one downstairs, just a lot of mess in the kitchen, and, from above, the sounds of music and shouting and laughter. Frowning, he went upstairs.

When the children had first put the light on in the attic room, Mum had carried on sleeping. Lucy put the tape recorder on the small, round table, and Will put the tray on the floor.

'Mum?' Lucy whispered. Mum grunted.

'You have to get up now, Mum,' Lucy whispered.

'Tell her it's her birthday,' Will said. 'She might have forgotten.'

Lucy told her.

Mum didn't move.

'Give her a little shake,' Will said.

Lucy gave her a shake, and Mum shrank deeper under the duvet.

'What shall I do, Will?' Lucy said.

'First you have to give her five minutes to come to,' Will said. 'And then you have to pull her duvet off.'

For the first time Mum spoke. 'Go away,' she said. She didn't move her mouth much, and she didn't open her eyes at all.

Lucy and Will whispered together.

'Perhaps we should give her one of the drinks straightaway,' Will said. 'That chocolatey one. It needs drinking. It's been in the cupboard a long time.'

'No,' Lucy said. She knew about shows, and she knew that you have to wait for half-time for drinks. 'First we have to do the dance,' she said. 'I think that might wake her up. Put the tape on, Will. Not too loud.'

Will wasn't sure which way to turn the
volume knob, but he turned it right round
to be on the safe side, and switched it on.

At once a noise like a high-speed train in
a tunnel filled the small room, and Mum
leapt upright in bed, with her eyes wide
open. Her mouth was wide open too,
though she didn't actually say anything.

'Oops,' Will said. 'Sorry.'

He turned the volume knob the other
way.

'Now, Will,' Lucy whispered
encouragingly.

'What?' he whispered back.

'Your dance,' Lucy whispered. 'Remember to smile,' she added.

Will gathered himself, took a little run across the room, leapt into the air with a confident smile, and smacked his head against the sloping part of the attic ceiling.

When Dad got to the top of the attic stairs, he stopped and peered round the door. He blinked. Mum was sitting up in bed, laughing and drinking something brown from a brandy glass, surrounded by several balloons, and the remains of balloons. Lucy, who was dressed in a lilac tutu and the top half of her bee costume, was dancing the cancan, and Will, dressed in his football kit, was crawling after her, miaowing.

As she danced, Lucy shrieked, 'A wolf! A wolf!'

Tchaikovsky blared from the tape machine. On the bed next to Mum, there was a tray with at least a dozen glasses on it filled with liquids of various colours.

Dad blinked again, and withdrew.

Mum began to clap to the music. Lucy span round three times, bowed elaborately, said, 'Oops, thought it'd finished,' and carried on spinning.

Will headed a balloon against a Velux window and shouted, 'Oh my god, it's a goal in the very last minute!'

Mum swallowed the last of the Cadbury's chocolate liqueur which had come free with a Christmas package of Dairy Milk the year before Will was born, and carried on clapping.

'Bravo!' she shouted. 'Bravo!' Her headache hadn't gone, but she wasn't thinking about it any more.

'Are you having a good birthday, Mum?' Lucy asked.

'I am,' Mum said. 'I don't quite know why or how. But I'm having a wonderful birthday. I don't see how it could be any better.'

Suddenly, from nowhere, Dad sprang into the room, and it got better. Mum choked. He was dressed in his blue-and-red-striped

dressing gown and a long blonde wig, and
he carried a wet and broken bunch of roses
in his mouth, and he high-kicked expertly
across the room, grunting in time to the
music.

'If we can't go to the ballet,' he panted,
trying not to chew the roses, 'the ballet must
come to us!' The children cheered, and as

the music came to an end with a roll of
drums, Dad and Will and Lucy linked arms

and performed an energetic
dance of their own invention,
and Mum rose from her
bed and applauded.

Afterwards, they all lay in
Mum and Dad's bed, and
recovered. Dad drank a
little of the drink from the
green bottle, which Will had mixed with
Ribena.

'It's quite nice,' he said. 'It's a bit like
eating very, very old sweets.'

'Pass me some more pitta bread,' Mum
said. 'It might have thawed by now.'

'Is this your best birthday ever, Mum?'
Lucy asked.

'Absolutely,' Mum said.

'What was the best bit of your best
birthday? Was it when Dad ate the flower?'

'That was a very good bit,' Mum said.
'But it was all good. It was good because

you're all so good.'

'Am *I*?' Lucy whispered.

'And Will,' Mum said.

Will looked up from *The Beano* at the sound of his name, and grunted.

'And,' Mum went on, 'I learned something very important this evening. Very important and very useful.'

'What did you learn?' Lucy asked.

'I learned what the quickest way to wake someone up is.'

Lucy smiled, but not very much. And without looking up from *The Beano*, Will said, 'I *told* you it was an awful day.'

Will

Will

It was nearly the end of August, and Timothy and Elizabeth were telling Will what they were getting for Christmas.

'The new Playstation,' Timothy said. 'Dad's promised.'

'A bicycle,' Elizabeth said. 'What are you getting, Will?'

Will, who hadn't thought about it, looked blank. They stared at him, shocked.

'Haven't you asked for anything yet?'

'Of course I have,' he said quickly.

'What?'

'A Harpy Eagle,' he said. It was the first thing that came into his head.

'What's a Harpy Eagle?'

'It's the dominant bird of prey in South America,' Will said.

 Will had always been interested in birds. Even when he was small he preferred Dad's copy of *Birds of the Western Palaearctic* to *Winnie-the-Pooh*. Facts about birds stuck in his head the way other things didn't. For instance, he could never remember where he'd left his gloves, but he remembered that smews live in holes in sandy banks. Although he'd never dreamed of actually owning a bird, the more he thought about it, the more he liked the idea. And a Harpy Eagle would be the ideal bird to begin with. By teatime he was impatient to let Mum and Dad know.

They were having cauliflower cheese, which Dad had made. Lucy hated Dad's cauliflower cheese. She stared at it angrily, as if trying to frighten it away.

'Eat half of it,' Mum said.

'I've been thinking,' Will said politely, 'about Christmas.'

'Christ Almighty,' Dad said. 'It's only August.'

Mum frowned. Dad said sorry.

Will tried again. 'You see, I'm not sure how long it takes to get what I want, so I thought I'd say now.'

'Very thoughtful,' Dad said. 'Come on, Poodlefish, you *have* to eat half.' Lucy snarled at the cauliflower cheese.

Will waited for them to ask him what he wanted, but they didn't.

'The reason for asking now,' he began again, but Dad interrupted him.

'Look,' Dad said. 'It's the middle of the summer. I'm not having any discussion about Christmas presents till December.'

'But I haven't even told you what . . .'

'No,' Dad said. 'And I mean no.' He used his angry voice. Dad could do angry quite well.

At school the following week, Will talked to Timothy again. They were walking round the edge of the field during afternoon break.

'How did you get your dad to promise to buy you the new Playstation for Christmas?' Will asked.

'Easy. He wants it too.'

'Oh.' Will thought about this. 'I don't think my dad would want a Harpy Eagle,' he said sadly.

'They say if I get into trouble I won't get the Playstation,' Timothy said. 'But I get into trouble anyway. Don't I, Will?'

Will nodded. Timothy was always getting into trouble.

'What did they say when you told them you wanted the Hippy Eagle?' Timothy asked.

'*Harpy* Eagle,' Will said. 'That's the problem. They won't listen. And if I try to tell them, I'll get told off for pestering.'

They walked right round the field, and when they got back to the classrooms, Will said, 'I know, I'll drop hints.' It was a phrase he'd heard Mum use.

'What do you mean?'

'I'll tell them without pestering.'

'How?'

'You know. Give them clues. Leave things round the house. Wink at them. That sort of thing. Mum said it's a way to get what you want without bother.'

'I like bother,' Timothy said.

When Will got home that afternoon, he had his glass of milk and piece of shortbread, and went straight up to his room, and shut the door. Apart from once, when he went into Dad's study to ask how to spell 'camouflage', Mum and Dad didn't see him until tea time. At tea he said hardly anything, and went back up to his room as soon as he could.

'What's the matter with Will?' Mum said.

Dad said, 'It's very odd. Earlier on, he kept winking at me.'

The following morning, when Dad went into his study, he found some sheets of paper on his chair. The sheets had been folded in half and stapled together to make a pamphlet. At the top of the front page was a headline – 'New Eagle Gazette' –

110

and, below, laid out like a newspaper, were
articles and pictures. It had been done on
the computer. The first article was headed:
'Birds of Prey'. Dad sat down and began to
read.

'Eagles are the biggest birds of prey.
Shrikes kill mice and sometimes rats, but
they are no bigger than starlings. Eagles are
the biggest of all meat-eaters. The South
American Harpy Eagle is even said to take
sloths which are as big as sheep dogs
hanging upside down in the Brazilian rain
forest.'

At teatime, Dad said to Will, 'I liked
your eagle newspaper, Will. Liked it very

much. Are you doing a project on eagles at school?'

'No,' said Will. 'Not that.' He said it in a mysterious way he'd practised, so Mum and Dad would know to ask him more.

'He's always been interested in birds,' Mum said. 'Ever since he was small. I think it's a lovely interest to have.'

'So do I,' Dad said. 'I wouldn't know a golden eagle from a silver one.'

'There's no such thing as a silver eagle,' Will said. They beamed at him and went on with their tea. Will caught Dad's eye and winked at him. Dad winked back. Will waited for him to say something, but he

didn't. He didn't say anything about eagles for the rest of the meal, he just finished his cheese and apple and asked Will to help clear the table.

Other boys might now have made the mistake of pestering, or else have given up, but Will was cleverer than that, and more cunning. His face went flat the way it did when he was very determined.

A week or so later, Mum came down to find an elaborate, brightly-coloured map in the back room showing all the birds of the Accipitridae family.

'That's nice,' she said. 'What's Accipitridae?'

'Eagles,' Will said.

'Your knowledge of birds is really impressive,' Mum said as she loaded the washing machine.

'There's one bird in particular I'm interested in,' Will said innocently.

'Really?'

'Yes.' When she didn't ask which it was, he said, 'Happens to be called the Harpy Eagle.'

Mum ran the taps to start the washing up, while Will waited for her to say something else.

'Does it sound like one?' she said eventually.

'*Harpy*,' Will said. 'Not harp.'

'Goodness, you know it all,' Mum said, and turned on the radio to catch the news.

A little later, Will saw Timothy in the playground.

'How's it going?' Timothy said.

'Not so good,' Will said. 'Dropping hints is a lot of work.'

'How much does the Hopping Eagle cost?' Timothy asked.

'*Harpy* Eagle. I don't know. About the same as the Playstation, I should think.'

'And how big is it?'

'Ninety centimetres from beak to tail.'

'Is that big?'

Will laughed. 'Of course it's big. It's enormous. It's the dominant bird of prey in the Brazilian rain forests.' Then he was silent. 'Maybe it's too big,' he said. 'Maybe Mum and Dad are worried about Lucy. She's frightened of big dogs. I didn't think of that. I'll have to ask for something smaller. Something friendlier to Lucy.'

Will was not only a determined boy, he was also adaptable and inventive.

First he tried macaws. Over the next couple of weeks, a carefully life-size papier maché model of a Hyacinth Macaw grew slowly in a corner of the back room.

'Isn't it a friendly size?' Will said to everyone who looked at it. Lucy helped by painting the macaw's left leg hot pink.

'You don't mind macaws, do you?' Will said to her. 'You like macaws.'

Lucy looked at it.

'I would,' she said, 'if they came in smaller sizes.'

Will switched to even smaller exotic birds: first parrots, then cockatoos, then parakeets and finally lovebirds. Throughout the autumn, pictures of each kept appearing in the back room, drawn to scale and shown in a well-stocked cage of the appropriate size, helpfully labelled 'seed-hopper', 'block of iodine', 'sprig of millet'.

No-one said anything, except for Lucy, who occasionally complained that he was using up all the Blu-tack.

One Sunday afternoon in November, feeling that time was running out, Will chanced a direct conversation about birds.

'Look at this Double-Eyed Fig Parrot,' he said to Dad, pointing to his picture. 'Small enough to fit into a deep pocket.' He stared at Dad in a meaningful way.

'Are you all right, Will? You look as if you're about to faint.'

'It's tame,' Will persisted. 'Gentle. Good with children. Especially younger sisters. Talks. Talks politely,' he added, thinking of the family rules.

'Extraordinary,' Dad said. 'Do you know, it's almost enough to make me reconsider our ban on pets.'

Will looked at him. 'What do you mean, ban on pets?'

'We agreed we wouldn't have any pets, last year, do you remember, when Lucy wanted a kitten. You were very determined not to have one. You said, "No pets in this house".'

Will tried hard not to remember.

'Does that mean I can't have a bird for Christmas?'

Dad put his hand on Will's shoulder and looked sympathetic. Dad could look very sympathetic when he wanted to.

Will sighed. 'Even at the beginning,' he said, 'I knew you'd never get me a Harpy Eagle.'

'Apparently they're very big,' Dad said. 'And monstrously ugly.'

Will was just about to be sad when Dad added, 'But Mum and I want to get you something very special this Christmas.'

'Something *very* special?'

'Something *extra* special. All this work, the New Eagle Gazette and the map and the pictures, has been fantastic.'

Will's grin was the exact opposite of his scowl, his whole face seemed to leap towards his hair. He began to talk in a rush. 'What is it, Dad? Is it expensive? Is it

big? Do you plug it in?'

'I can't say. It's a surprise.' Dad looked firm. He didn't do firm as well as he did friendly or sympathetic, but Will could tell he wasn't going to say.

'Aw, *Dad*!' he said, looking very pleased.

During the last few weeks of the winter term, Will was in a very good mood. He told Timothy that his Christmas present was finally sorted out.

'What?' Timothy said. 'The Barmy Eagle?'

'*Harpy* Eagle. No, not that. That was a long time ago. But something special. Dad said.'

'Didn't your hints work then?'

'Well,' Will said. 'In a way, they did. I'm not getting a Harpy Eagle, but it's because of the hints I'm getting something extra special. They're funny things, hints. Or maybe it's just mums and dads. What about your Playstation?'

Timothy shook his head gloomily. 'Ever

since I got into trouble last week, they keep going on about me having to be good. I told them I *always* put Liam's head down the toilet when he's like that, it's not being bad, it's just being normal, but they don't care about being normal, they just care about being good. They say if I get into trouble again, just once, for anything at all, they'll take away my Playstation and give it to someone deserving. That's what they keep on saying.'

'What are you going to do?'

'I don't know.' Timothy thought about it, but after a long time he gave up and shook his head again. 'I can't think of anything,'

he said. 'I might even have to be good. I might have to be good *for a whole month.*' His voice was dismal.

Will patted him on the shoulder. He felt very mellow now that his own present was sorted out. 'I'll help you,' he said. 'Don't worry, Tim, I'll help you get your Playstation.'

At home, Will asked Mum if Timothy's dad was really going to take away his Christmas present if he got into trouble again.

'It wasn't just a bit of trouble Timothy got into,' Mum said. 'It was serious. His name went into the book.'

'Oh,' Will said.

Having your name put in the book was the worst punishment possible at Parkside School. First you were sent to see Miss Strickland, the headmistress. Everyone was frightened of her, even the other teachers. She had a big meaty face which shook when she shouted. Even more frightening, she couldn't say the letter r; she made a whirring noise instead. After she had shouted at you, she wrote your name down in her book with all the other very naughty children's names, and then after that – and this was the worst thing of all – she phoned your mum and dad and told them what you'd done.

'That's why,' Mum said. 'It's serious when Miss Strickland phones you.'

Will shivered. 'Yes, I see,' he said.

The winter term at school was always the hardest term, and the last two weeks were the hardest part of the hardest term. There was the carol concert to practise for, and

the winter fête to organize, and the hall decorations to put up, and the Christmas show to put on. This winter, things were even harder than usual: several members of staff were ill with flu, and everything was running late. The weather was wet, and the children were badly behaved. Miss Strickland shouted and whirred, and there was an outbreak of swine fever among the guinea pigs.

Will walked with Timothy round the field. Timothy had developed a slight twitch in his left eye.

'It's hard being good, isn't it?' Will said conversationally. 'I didn't know being good all the time was so hard.'

'I didn't know what being good was *like*,' Timothy said. 'Liam tied my shoelaces together the other day, and I had to pretend I didn't know it was him.' His eye twitched. 'You should have seen the look he gave me. He thinks I've gone *soft*.'

'Think of the Playstation,' Will said. 'That's all you've got to do.'

Timothy muttered to himself.

A week went by, and the end of the term was almost on them.

Every day, Will and Timothy walked round the field. 'You can do it, Tim,' Will said. 'You're going to do it.' He used a kindly, encouraging voice, which somehow reminded him of Mum and Dad. 'You're nearly there.'

The last event of the last day of term was the Christmas show, a story of love and fellowship throughout the world. It had been written by Mr Sheringham, and contained walk-on parts for figures from all of history. Will was Sir Isaac Newton and Timothy was William Shakespeare. Will had to say, 'So say I, Sir Isaac Newton, discoverer of gravity,' and Timothy had to say, 'So say I, William Shakespeare, great English playwright.' In rehearsals they rarely managed to say these things – they said, 'So say I, Sir Isaac Newton, discoverer of gravy,' or 'So say I, William Shakespeare, discoverer of Sir Isaac Newton.' But most of their time was spent waiting backstage for their turn to come on.

Because other teachers were still off sick,

Mr Sheringham had to organize all the
rehearsals and make all the scenery on his
own, and day by day he grew more and
more anxious and cross, and by the day of
the performance, he'd changed from a
short, neat person wearing a tie, to a wet-
faced man with staring eyes and half a

beard. Sometimes he spoke in a fierce
whisper, sometimes in a bullish bellow.
Neither had any effect on the children,
who, just a few days away from Christmas,
were boisterous and larky.

On the day of the performance, Will and Timothy waited backstage to go on. All around them there was uproar as the other children, fed up with their costumes and bored by the constant delays, bickered and fought.

'I hate William Shakespeare,' Timothy said gloomily. 'Shakespeare's making this very difficult for me.' His eye now twitched continuously.

'Easy,' Will said. 'Almost there.'

'I just hope no-one gets in my way.'

'Think *Playstation*,' Will said. 'Say it after me. Playstation.'

'Playstation,' Timothy said. 'Playstation. Playstation.' His eye twitched.

The show dragged on. Backstage, the children got rowdier and rowdier. Mr Sheringham ran in wet-faced to tell them to be quiet. His voice cracked as he spoke to them.

'There are mums and dads out there,' he said. Someone at the back cackled.

After he went there was silence for a few minutes, and then a slowly increasing murmur began. A paper ball hit the wall above Timothy's head, and he looked round angrily.

For the second time, Mr Sheringham came back-stage, hissing furiously at everyone to be quiet. But as soon as he'd gone,

another paper ball hit Timothy on the top of the head. And that did it.

'Liam!' Timothy shouted, standing up.

Will pulled him back down, but he struggled free and stood up again, and a hail of paper balls came flying across the room. Then a duffel bag. It looped across the room and hit Timothy on the side of his head, and knocked him over. He scrambled up and piled across the room, and Will dived after him.

'No!' he shouted. 'Tim, don't!'

Launching himself, he brought him down a few feet from Liam, and they rolled on the floor, everyone else screaming round them.

And then there was silence.

Mr Sheringham was small and square. Will hadn't expected him to have such powerful arms. He lifted both Will and Timothy off the ground, and carried them out of the room into the corridor. He was bright red and very wet with anger. Apart from the low sound of voices in the hall

where, despite everything, the show was continuing, there was silence. Timothy and Will said nothing, but Timothy was twitching badly, Will could see his face pulling itself out of shape.

'Who's responsible for this commotion?' Mr Sheringham hissed. 'Is it you, Peachey?'

Timothy twitched. He saw Liam in the doorway, and made a movement as if he were about to charge past Mr Sheringham towards him, when Will said, 'No, it was me.' It happened so fast, he'd said it before realizing that he was doing it to save Timothy's Playstation.

Mr Sheringham put his face very close to Will's.

'Quigley,' he said. His expression was oddly twisted, as if he'd just eaten something very hot, and there was a sort of astonishment in his voice.

'Go and wait in Miss Strickland's office, Quigley,' he said. 'I'm going to fetch her.'

'But,' Will said.

'We'll do without Newton in this show,'

Mr Sheringham said. 'I never liked Newton. Listen to me, Quigley. Miss Strickland's in a very bad mood today, and I don't think she's ever been as cross as she's going to be with you.'

At that moment Will realized what he'd done. The thought of his Extra-Special Christmas Present came briefly into his head, and at once disappeared.

From behind Mr Sheringham, Timothy said, 'No, wait a minute! Wait!' but Mr Sheringham rounded on him and pushed him back along the corridor, and Will turned and went down the corridor alone towards Miss Strickland's office.

He was in bed that night when Miss Strickland rang. He was lying awake, and he heard Mum answer the phone. He heard her say, 'Oh, hello, Miss Strickland.' And then he heard her say, 'Oh dear. I'm very sorry to hear that.' He'd known straightaway that he was done for. He was already out of bed with his dressing-gown on, when Mum came up to his room to fetch him.

He stood in the back room in his dressing-gown, trying to explain what had happened. It was a very difficult thing to explain. He couldn't say why he had attacked Timothy, or Timothy would lose his Playstation. On the other hand, if he didn't say why he'd attacked Timothy, he might not get his own Special Christmas Present. But the more he thought about it, the more determined he was not to let Timothy down. His face went flat.

'Why, Will?' Mum said, for the fifth time. Will shook his head again.

'Well, what did Miss Strickland say to you?' Mum asked.

'She was cross.'

'I bet she was,' Dad said grimly. 'And what did she say?'

'She told me off.' His voice was very quiet by now.

'Speak up, Will. What did she actually say?'

'Well,' he said slowly, screwing up his face as if trying to remember something from many years earlier. 'She was shouting. And her face did the shaking thing. And she was making the whirring noise. And . . .'

Mum said. 'Did your name go in the book?'

Will looked at his feet and didn't say anything.

'Did it, Will?'

He nodded.

Dad gave a moan, and swore, and Mum didn't tell him off. Dad began to work himself up into a temper. Dad could get into quite a temper if he wanted to.

'Please, don't take away my Extra-Special Christmas Present!' Will said quietly.

This only made Mum angrier. 'You shouldn't think so much about yourself,' she said. 'I've never known you so selfish, Will.'

'Now go to bed,' Dad said. 'Before you make it any worse.'

But it wasn't clear how it could be any worse.

Christmas Eve should have been a wonderful day. But Will couldn't do anything without cool, disappointed looks from Mum and Dad. He wanted to talk to them one last time about his Extra-Special Christmas Present, but he could never work

out exactly what he'd say, and besides, they wouldn't let him start. They just gave him cool, disappointed looks. He got the looks while they were wrapping presents, he got them while they were hanging up their stockings, and he got them while they were putting out mince pies and mulled wine for Father Christmas and a carrot for Rudolf. Once he overheard them talking about him. Mum was saying things like, 'I can't understand it.' And Dad said, 'Well, I think we're doing the right thing.' Eventually he was so miserable, he went and sat on his bed, not doing anything, not even reading *The Beano*.

Lucy came up to see him.

'Aren't you getting a Christmas present, Will?' she asked.

He didn't say anything.

'Why aren't you getting a Christmas present, Will?'

He just shook his head again.

Lucy said, 'You can have one of mine if you want, Will. Do you want one, Will? If

I get more than one Barbie, you can have the other one. I promise. I'm not lying.'

Will lay down on the bed, and Lucy went because she didn't want to see him cry.

As soon as she'd got downstairs, there was a knock on the front door, and when she answered it she found Timothy standing on the doorstep. Timothy looked very awkward. He was carrying a crumpled plastic carrier bag which seemed to be empty.

'I don't think Will wants to play,' Lucy said. She looked at the bag, wondering what sort of game you could play with an empty carrier bag.

Timothy shuffled around a bit, then he said in a low, gruff voice, 'I'd better see your mum and dad.'

Dad went to the door. 'Come in, Timothy,' he said.

But Timothy stayed at the door. He seemed to be having problems with the bag.

He moved it from one hand to the other, and then suddenly, without saying anything, gave it to Dad.

'For me?' Dad asked.

'Sort of,' Timothy said.

'Is there anything in it?' Dad said, holding it. 'Or is it just the bag? It's quite a nice bag,' he added, as if not wanting to hurt Timothy's feelings.

'It's inside,' Timothy said.

By this time, Mum was at the front door too, and they all watched while Dad put his hand in the bag, felt round for some time, and eventually pulled out a rather bent and grimy twenty pound note, which he examined in astonished silence.

'Twenty pounds,' Timothy said, in case Dad didn't recognize it.

Dad said, 'Um.' He looked up the street to see if Ben was on his way.

'I didn't steal it,' Timothy said. 'It's for Will's present. To buy off you the present you're not giving Will so I can give it to him. The Barmy Eagle or whatever.'

141

Dad turned to Mum and made a gesture to show that he was out of his depth.

'Isn't it enough?' Timothy said.

Moving in front of Dad, Mum said, 'We don't understand, Timothy. Why do you want to buy Will's present?'

Timothy looked even more awkward at

this point, he stood there with his head down, and when he eventually lifted it, he said loudly, 'You tell them, Will!' And Mum and Dad and Lucy turned round to find Will standing on the stairs behind them.

'Will?' Dad said. 'What's all this about?'

'Well,' said Will, looking embarrassed. 'It's partly about Tim's Playstation. And it's partly about trying to be good for too long.'

On Christmas Day morning, after breakfast
was finished, Will and Lucy lined up outside
the living room, where the presents were.
First Lucy was in front, then Will was.
Then, after she'd stopped crying and Will
had said sorry, Lucy was again.

'OK,' Mum said. 'In you go.'

Lucy dashed in so fast she almost collided with the biggest, brightest play-kitchen she'd ever seen. She stood there, looking at it, and looking at Mum and Dad, and looking back at it, and grinning.

Will didn't go in straightaway. He stood in the doorway very calmly, looking at everything at once, the huge pile of wrapped presents under the tree, the half-eaten mince-pie and nibbled carrot in the fireplace, the biggest, brightest play-kitchen Lucy had ever seen, and the box on the coffee table covered with two faded towels. So this is Christmas, he thought, and after all the ups and downs of the last few months he felt it was something outside himself, to be thought about, not rushed into.

And then the box on the coffee table covered with two faded towels made a noise. *Natter-natter.*

Will stood in the doorway, not breathing.

The box under the towels made another noise, *tuckle-tuckle-tuckle*, and Will walked up

to it, and took off the towels. Underneath was a large wire cage, and in the cage were two birds, one blue and one green, cleaning their beaks and peering out at him.

'Budgerigars,' Will said softly, almost to himself. And because he was confused, he said shyly, 'Who are they for?'

Mum and Dad were grinning.

'But I thought,' he began. 'What you said about pets,' he began again. But he was distracted. 'Wild Budgerigars come from in Australia,' he said, interrupting himself. 'They live in flocks and nest in sandy holes.'

'I thought you'd know something like that,' Dad said.

'You only get green and yellow ones in the wild. Never blue.' He put his hand into the cage and the blue budgerigar immediately hopped onto his finger. He looked at Dad. 'They're beautiful. I think they're more beautiful than Harpy Eagles,' he said.

'Those ugly birds!' Dad said. 'I could tell you what I think of Harpy Eagles.'

But Mum wouldn't let him. Instead they all sat on the sofa and ate chocolates and Will told them again about Mr Sheringham and his wet face, and Miss Strickland's whirring and shouting, until Timothy came round and asked if Will could come and be the first to play on his new Playstation.

The End

Dad

Mum

um

Lucy

Will

Dad

Mum

m

Lucy

Will